Full STEAM Ahead!

Technology Time

Technology and You!

Cynthia O'Brien

Crabtree Publishing

crabtreebooks.com

Title-Specific Learning Objectives:

Readers will:

- Understand that a technology is a tool that makes life easier, safer, and more fun.
- Identify and explain some of the technologies that people rely on each day.
- Ask and answer questions about how they use technology each day.

High-frequency words (grade one)	Academic vocabulary
and, is, it, make, the, they, this, to, use	gather, information, protect, technology

Before, During, and After Reading Prompts:

Activate Prior Knowledge and Make Predictions:

Have children read the title and look at the images on the cover and title page.

Activate interest and prior knowledge by giving statements and having children show you a thumbs-up if they agree or a thumbs-down if they disagree.

Statements could include:

- The girl on the cover is using technology.
- A school bus is an example of technology.
- Technology is only digital devices.
- Technology is all around us.

During Reading: After reading pages 18 and 19, ask children to think about the technologies they use in different weather. Ask them:

- What technologies do you see on these pages? How do they protect people in different weather?
- What is the weather like today? Did you use or wear any technologies to protect you?

After Reading:

Discuss the technologies that children use each day. Invite children to create technology timelines that identify and illustrate all of the technologies they use from morning to night.

Crabtree Publishing

crabtreebooks.com 800-387-7650

Hardcover 978-0-7787-6202-7
Paperback 978-0-7787-6239-3
Ebook (pdf) 978-1-4271-2258-2

Printed in Canada/032024/CP20240326

Library and Archives Canada Cataloguing in Publication

O'Brien, Cynthia (Cynthia J.), author
Technology and you! / Cynthia O'Brien.

(Full STEAM ahead!)
Includes index.
Issued in print and electronic formats.
ISBN 978-0-7787-6202-7 (hardcover).--
ISBN 978-0-7787-6239-3 (softcover).--
ISBN 978-1-4271-2258-2 (HTML)
1. Technology--Juvenile literature. 2. Inventions--Juvenile literature.
I. Title.

T48.O275 2019 C2018-906162-6

Published in Canada
Crabtree Publishing
616 Welland Avenue
St. Catharines, Ontario
L2M 5V6

Published in the United States
Crabtree Publishing
347 Fifth Avenue
Suite 1402-145
New York, NY 10016

Author: Cynthia O'Brien
Series Development: Reagan Miller
Editor: Janine Deschenes
Proofreader: Melissa Boyce
STEAM Notes for Educators: Janine Deschenes
Guided Reading Leveling: Publishing Solutions Group
Cover, Interior Design, and Prepress: Samara Parent
Photo research: Cynthia O'Brien and Samara Parent
Production coordinator: Katherine Kantor
Photographs: iStock: FamVeld: p. 19 (top); vitapix: p. 20
All other photographs by Shutterstock

Library of Congress Cataloging-in-Publication Data

Names: O'Brien, Cynthia, author.
Title: Technology and you! / Cynthia O'Brien.
Description: New York, New York : Crabtree Publishing, 2019. |
Series: Full STEAM ahead! | Includes index.
Identifiers: LCCN 2018056588 (print) |
LCCN 2018056891 (ebook) |
ISBN 9781427122582 (Electronic) |
ISBN 9780778762027 (hardcover : alk. paper) |
ISBN 9780778762393 (pbk. : alk. paper)
Subjects: LCSH: Technology--Juvenile literature. |
Tools--Juvenile literature.
Classification: LCC T48 (ebook) | LCC T48 .O27 2019 (print) |
DDC 600--dc23
LC record available at https://lccn.loc.gov/2018056588

Table of Contents

Technology Everywhere

You use or see **technology** all day.
It makes your life easier, safer, and more fun.

A scooter is a technology that makes life more fun! A helmet is a technology that makes life safer.

You start using technology when your day begins.

Your toothbrush is a technology that makes it easier to clean your teeth.

In the Kitchen

Time to eat! Look around the kitchen. What technologies do you see?

A refrigerator keeps food cold. It helps food stay **fresh** and safe to eat.

Bowls, spoons, and cups are technologies. They make it easier to eat food. What other technologies do you use to eat?

Wearing Technology

You wear technology too! Shoes and boots are technologies. Hats and glasses are technologies.

Shoes **protect** your feet. They make it easier to run and jump.

Boots keep your feet warm and dry in rain or snow.

Glasses help some people see more easily.

Going to School

You use technology to help you get to school.

A school bus makes it easier for children to get to school. One school bus can fit many children!

Some children ride bicycles to school. How do you get to school?

A backpack is a technology that helps you carry things to school.

At School

At school, there are technologies that help you learn and have fun.

Books make learning easier. They have **information** you can read. They are fun to read too!

Pens and mouse pads are technologies too. What other technologies are at your school?

Outdoor Fun

Do you play any games? Technology makes games easier, safer, and more fun.

Skates make it easier to move on ice.

People use a ball and a stick to play **lacrosse**. They wear helmets and body pads to stay safe.

Outdoor Jobs

Backyards and parks are fun places to play. Technologies help us take care of them.

A lawn mower helps us cut grass.

A garden shovel helps us plant flowers.

In fall, leaves drop from trees. A rake helps us gather the leaves. Do you help to do any outdoor jobs?

Different Weather

You use technology to help you in different **weather**.

You might wear a hat in sunny weather. It protects your eyes and skin from the **bright** Sun.

An umbrella helps keep you dry in rainy weather.

Gloves help keep your hands warm in cold weather.

Seeing at Night

At night, it becomes dark outside. Technology helps us see at night! This makes life easier and safer.

A light bulb is a technology. It lights up the rooms in our homes.

Have you ridden in a car at night? Many roads have streetlights. Cars have headlights. These help drivers see. They make driving at night safer.

Words to Know

bright [brahyt] adjective Shining or giving off a lot of light

fresh [fresh] adjective New; not spoiled or stale

information [in-fer-MEY-shuhn] noun Knowledge passed on in writing or by talking

lacrosse [luh-KROS] noun A team game in which players use sticks to shoot a ball into a net

protect [pruh-TEKT] verb To keep from being hurt

technology [tek-NOL-uh-jee] noun The tools that help us do work

weather [WETH-er] noun How it is outside, for example, if it is raining or sunny

A noun is a person, place, or thing.

A verb is an action word that tells you what someone or something does.

An adjective is a word that tells you what something is like.

Index

About the Author

Cynthia O'Brien has written many books for young readers. It is fun to help make a technology like a book! Books can be full of stories. They also teach you about the world around you, including other technologies.

To explore and learn more, enter the code at the Crabtree Plus website below.

www.crabtreeplus.com/fullsteamahead

Your code is:
fsa20

STEAM Notes for Educators

Full STEAM Ahead is a literacy series that helps readers build vocabulary, fluency, and comprehension while learning about big ideas in STEAM subjects. *Technology and You!* uses clear examples to encourage readers to ask and answer questions about how they use technology each day. The STEAM activity below helps readers extend the ideas in the book to build their skills in technology and arts.

A Day of Technology

Children will be able to:

- Identify some technologies that they use or see every day.
- Create a comic strip that shows them using technology throughout their day.

Materials

- Comic Strip Planning Sheet
- Comic Strip Template
- Art materials such as crayons or pencil crayons, stickers, markers, etc.

Guiding Prompts

After reading *Technology and You!*, ask children:

- What is technology?
- Can you think of some examples of technologies that you use each day? (Make a list of some examples to inspire children during their activity.)

Activity Prompts

Remind children that from morning to evening, they use technology all day! They will display the technology they use in a fun way by creating a comic strip.

Hand children the Comic Strip Planning Sheet. Review the criteria with children.

Their comic strips must have:

- Six pictures representing the progression of the day, with a minimum of one morning, one afternoon, and one evening.
- Text bubbles in each picture. Place some examples on the board for reference, such as:
    - Yawn! That alarm clock is LOUD!
    - I almost forgot my backpack!
    - The swings are my favorite!
    - Good thing I have my eraser...
    - Mmm. My favorite dinner!
    - Brush away the day!

When children have completed their planning sheet, they can create a good copy on the template. Put the good copies together into a class booklet. Laminate the pages or scan them and create a digital booklet.

Extensions

- Invite children to turn their comic strips into a short performance of their choice, such as a play, a series of tableaus, or a puppet show.

To view and download the worksheets, visit **www.crabtreebooks.com/resources/printables** or **www.crabtreeplus.com/fullsteamahead** and enter the code **fsa20**.